MEET MS. MARVEL

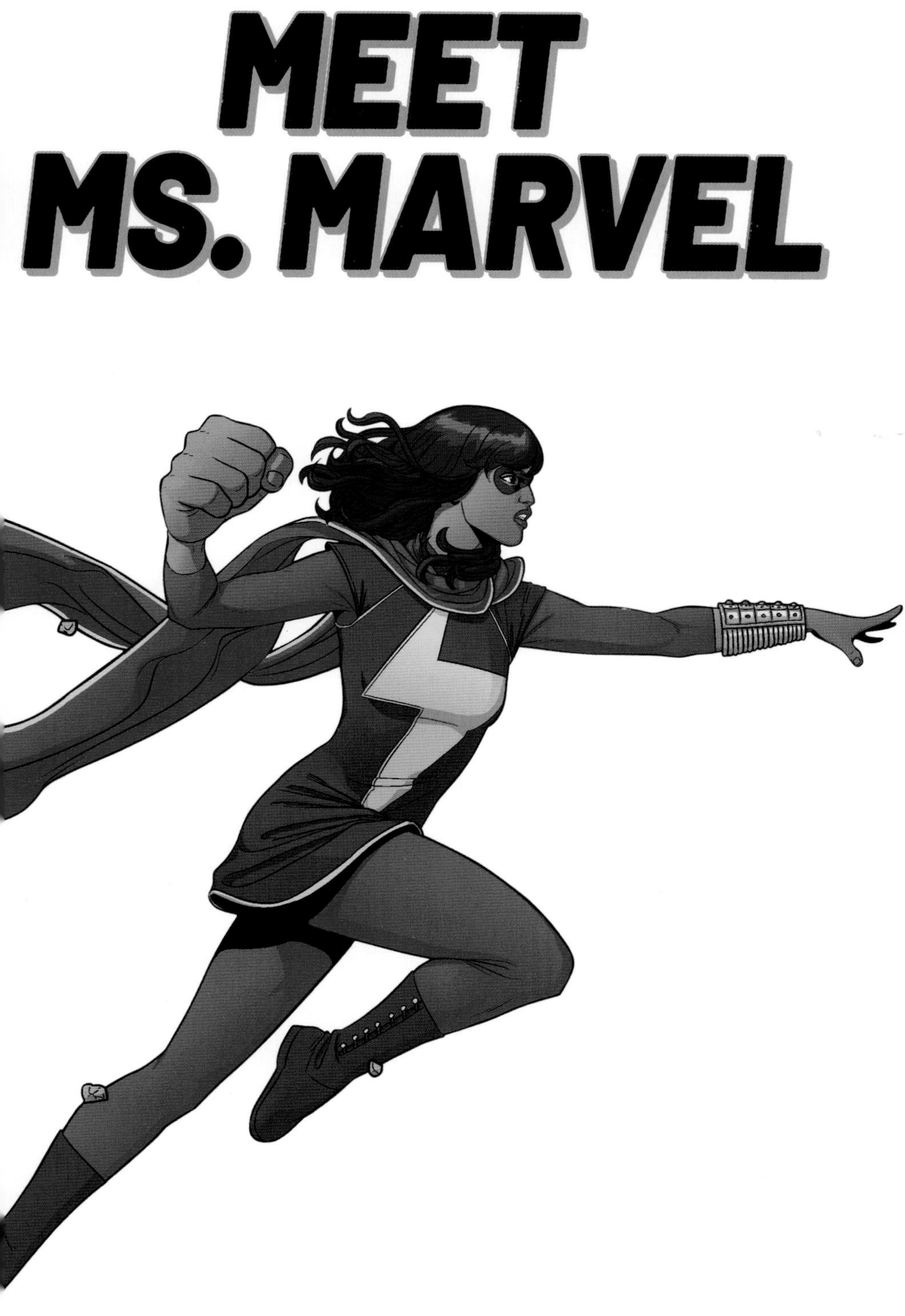

Penguin
Random
House

Project Editor Pamela Afram
Project Art Editor Jon Hall
Designer Thelma-Jane Robb
Proofreader Julia March
Senior Production Editor Marc Staples
Senior Production Controller Mary Slater
Managing Editor Emma Grange
Managing Art Editor Vicky Short
Publishing Director Mark Searle

First American Edition, 2023
Published in the United States by DK Publishing
1745 Broadway, 20th Floor, New York, NY 10019

DK, a Division of Penguin Random House LLC
23 24 25 26 27 10 9 8 7 6 5 4 3 2 1
001–333135–Jan /2023

© 2023 MARVEL

A catalog record for this book is available from the Library of Congress.
ISBN: 978-0-7440-7062-0 (Paperback)
ISBN: 978-0-7440-7063-7 (Hardcover)

DK books are available at special discounts when purchased in bulk for sales promotions,
premiums, fund-raising, or educational use. For details, contact: DK Publishing Special Markets,
1745 Broadway, 20th Floor, New York, NY 10019
SpecialSales@dk.com

Printed and bound in China

For the curious
www.dk.com

MIX
Paper | Supporting
responsible forestry
FSC™ C018179

This book is made from
Forest Stewardship Council™
certified paper—one small
step in DK's commitment
to a sustainable future.

Level 3

Meet Ms. Marvel

Pamela Afram

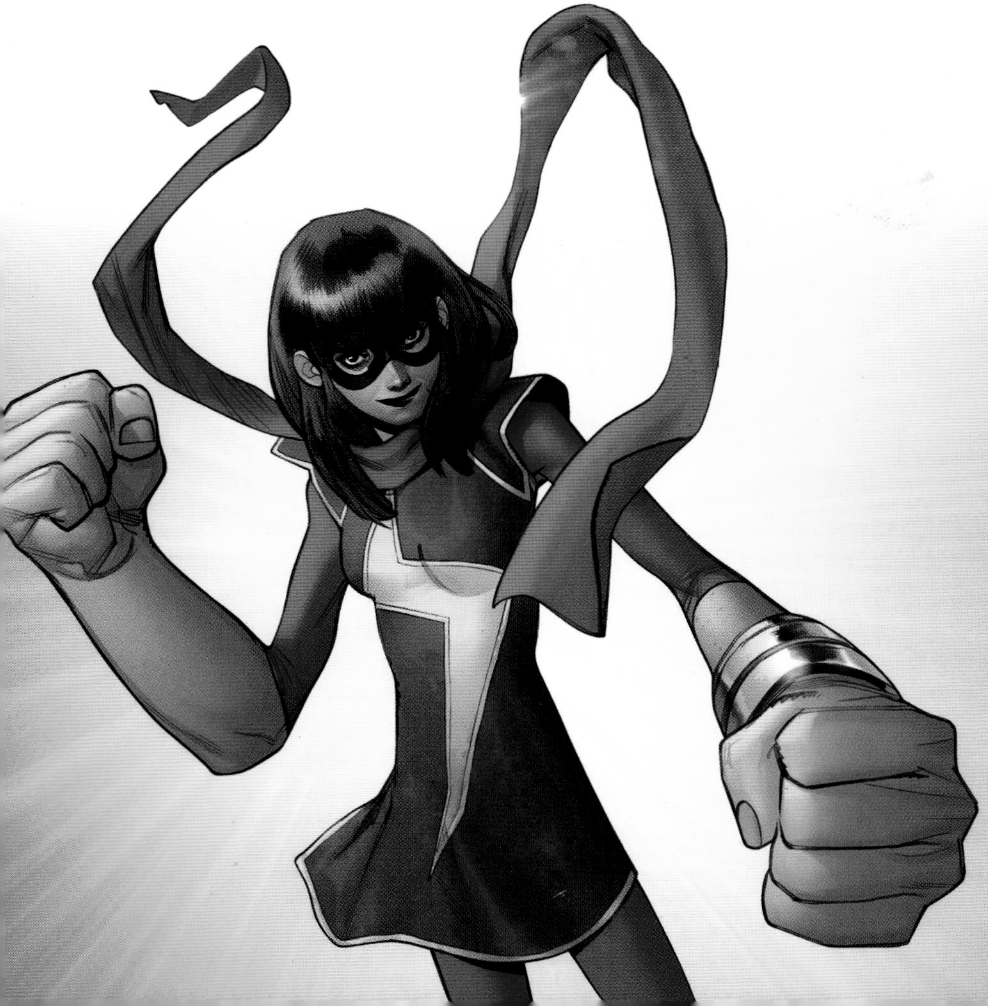

Contents

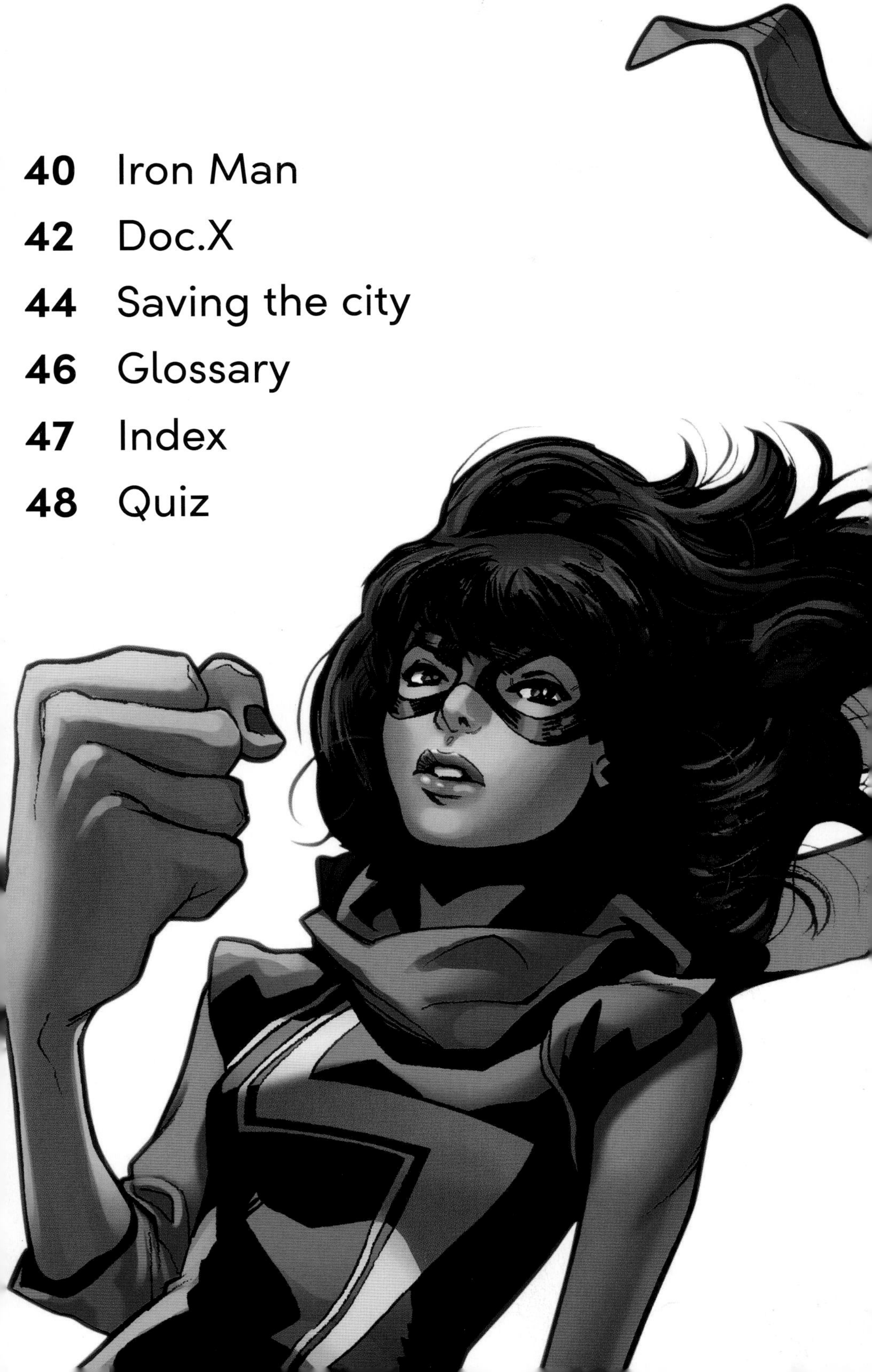

Meet Kamala Khan

Kamala Khan is a teenager with a special secret. She is also the Super Hero named Ms. Marvel! Kamala has amazing powers. She can stretch her body into any shape or size.

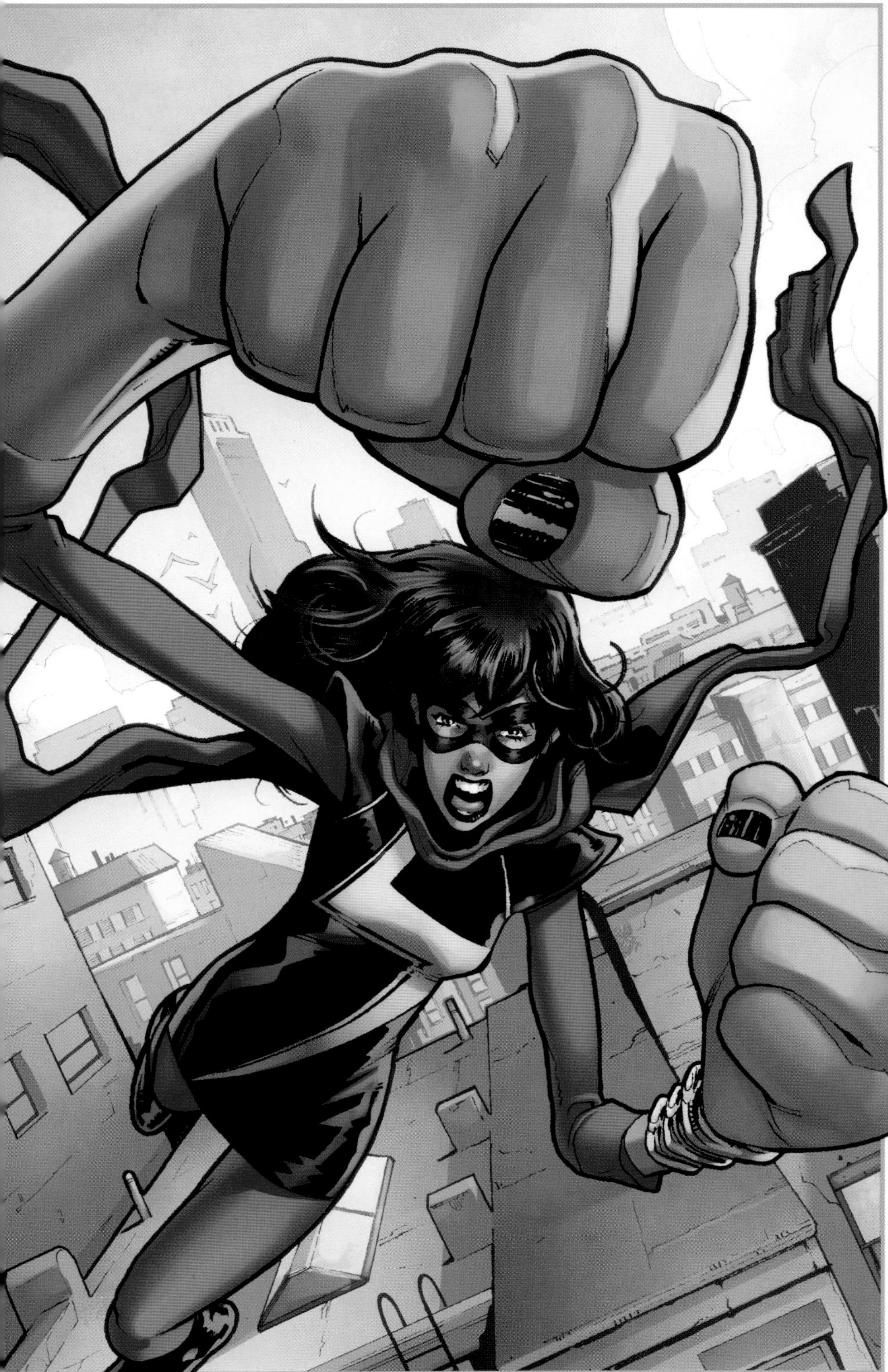

An extraordinary teenager

It is not easy being a teenage Super Hero. Kamala has to battle monsters and save the world. She also has to finish her homework and get to school on time!

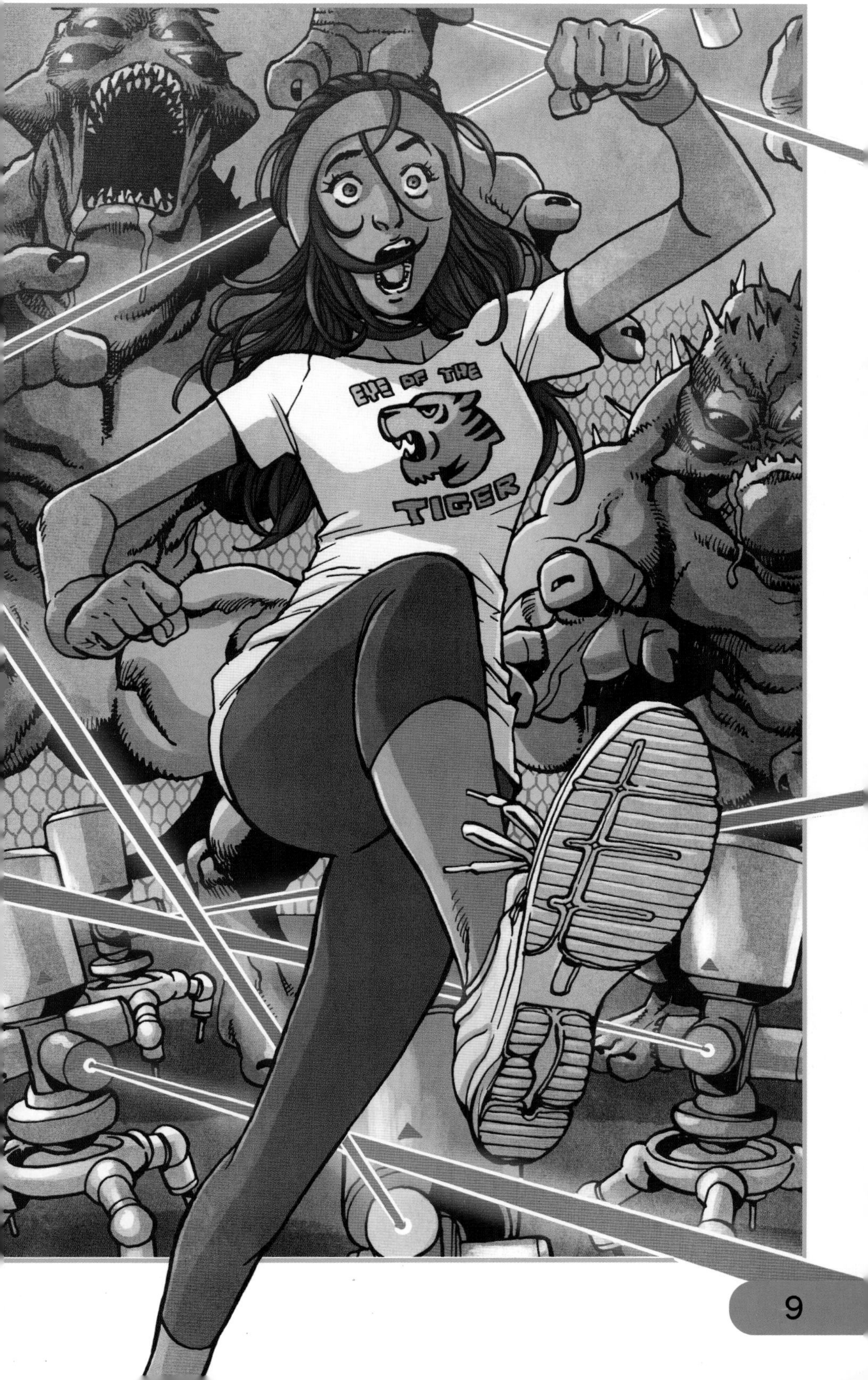
EYE OF THE
TIGER

Terrigen Mist

On the way home from a party, Kamala was engulfed in a mysterious mist. The mist knocked Kamala unconscious. When she recovered, she had amazing super-powers!

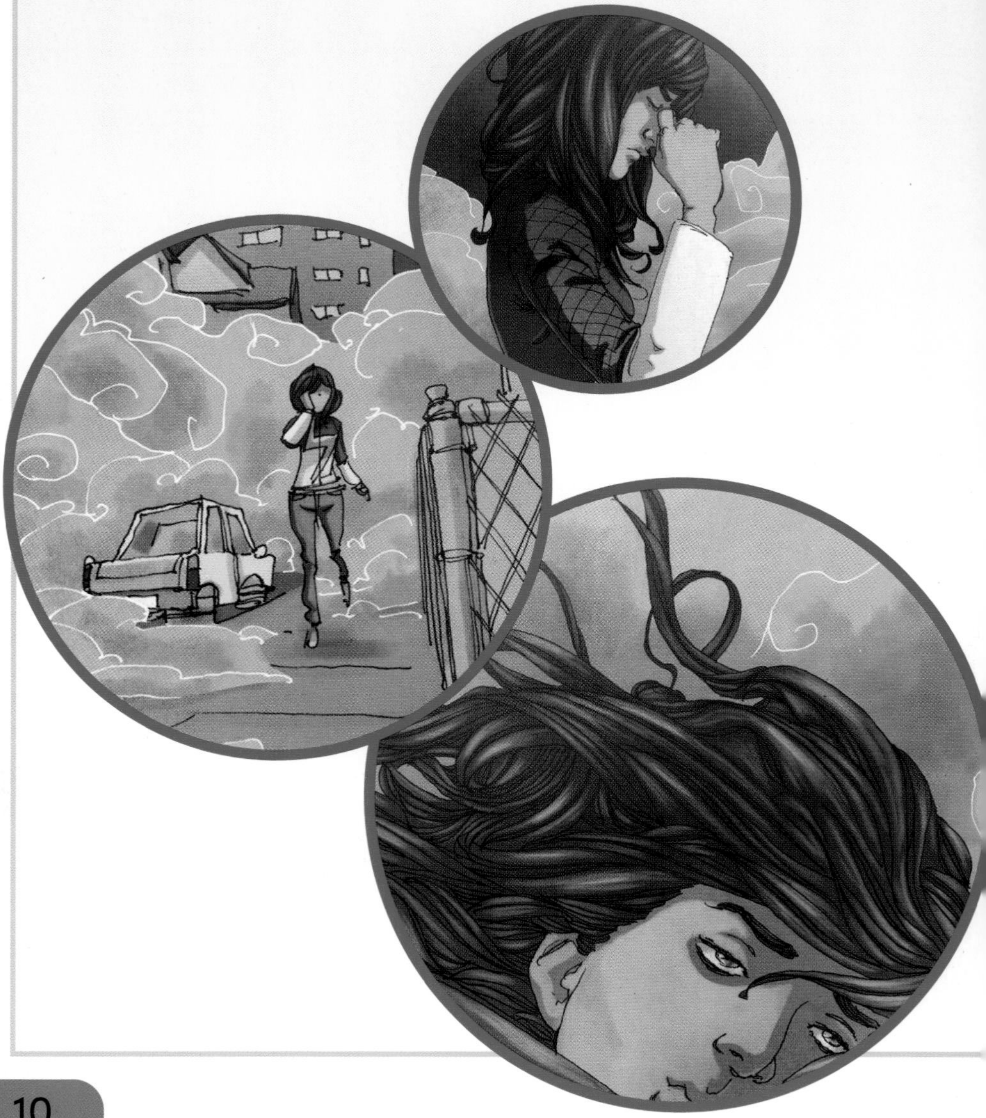

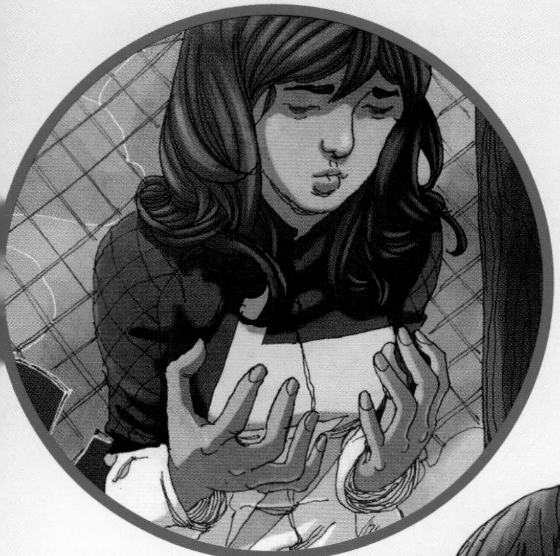

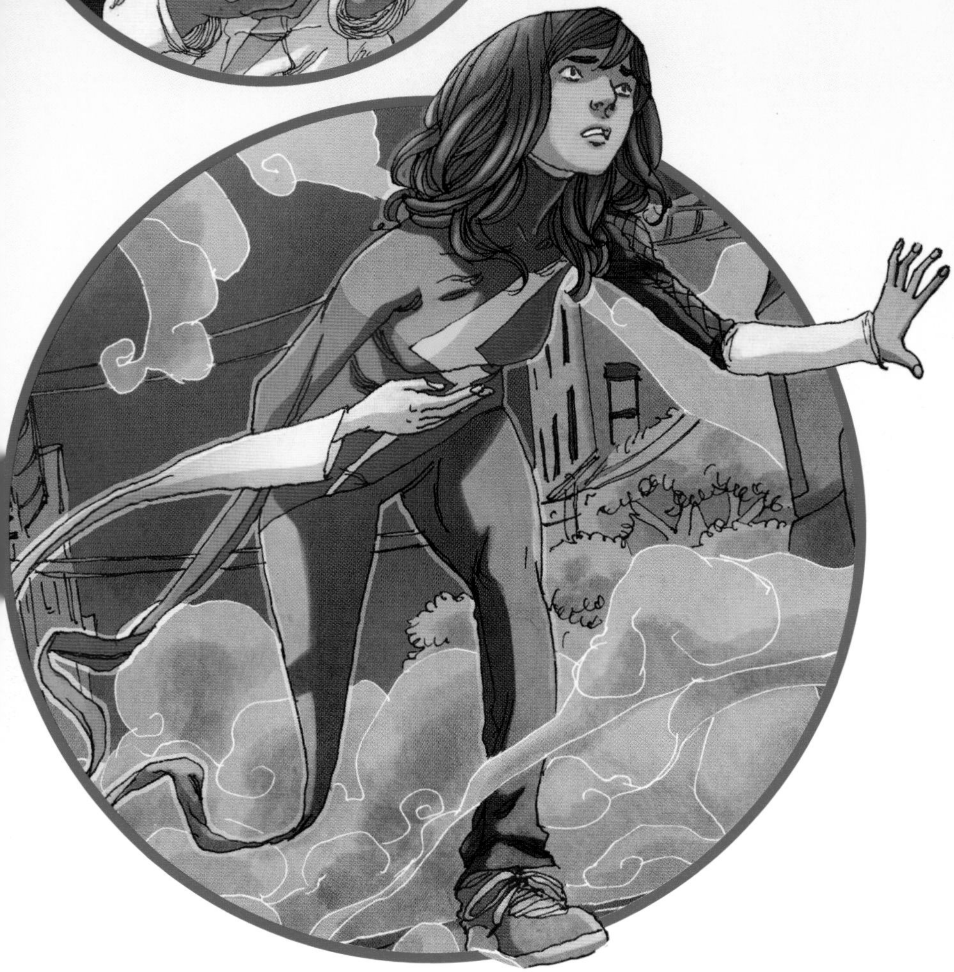

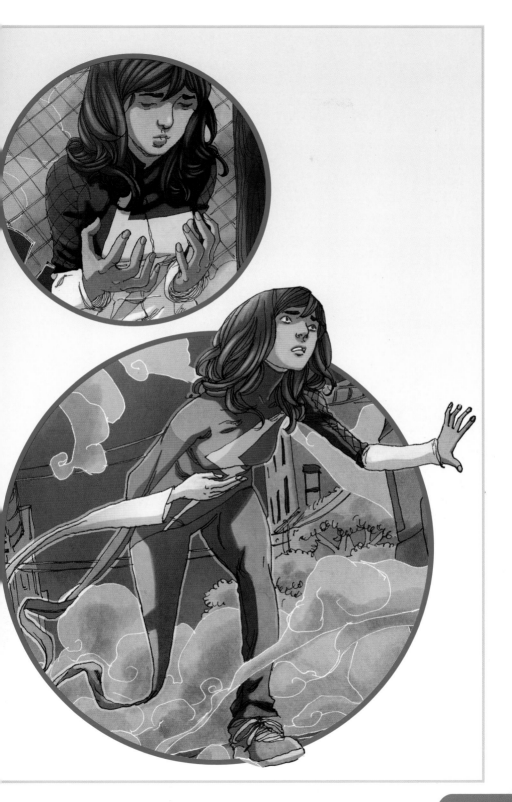

Kamala's powers

Kamala can change her shape and size. Her amazing super-powers allow her to do fantastic things.

Growth
Kamala can make her fists really big and smash through things in her way.

Shape-shifting
She can turn her body into steps to help people escape.

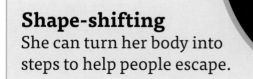

Strength
Kamala is really strong and can grow to an incredible size.

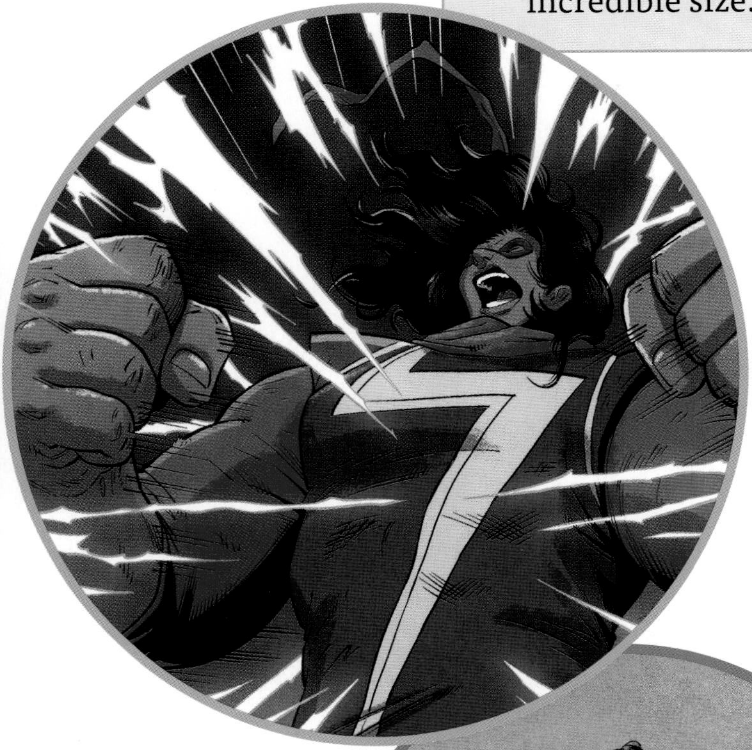

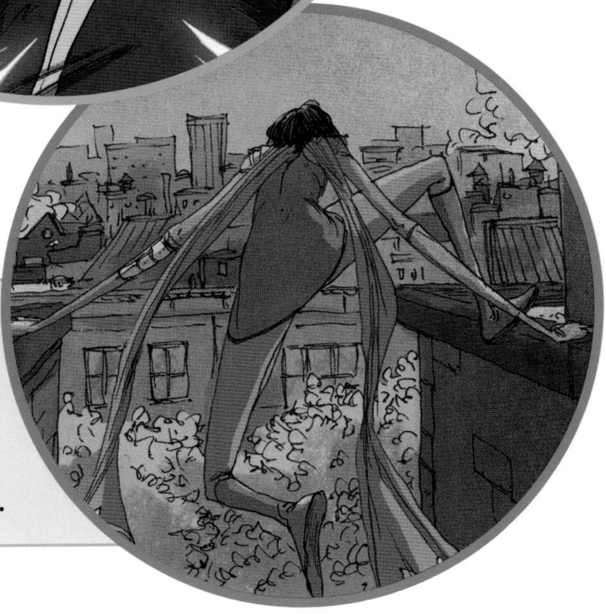

Stretchable
She can extend her arms and legs so she can climb between buildings.

Lockjaw

Kamala has a pet dog called Lockjaw. Lockjaw looks like a regular dog, but he is really an Inhuman with special powers. Lockjaw can teleport Kamala to any location. He protects Kamala and helps her in battles.

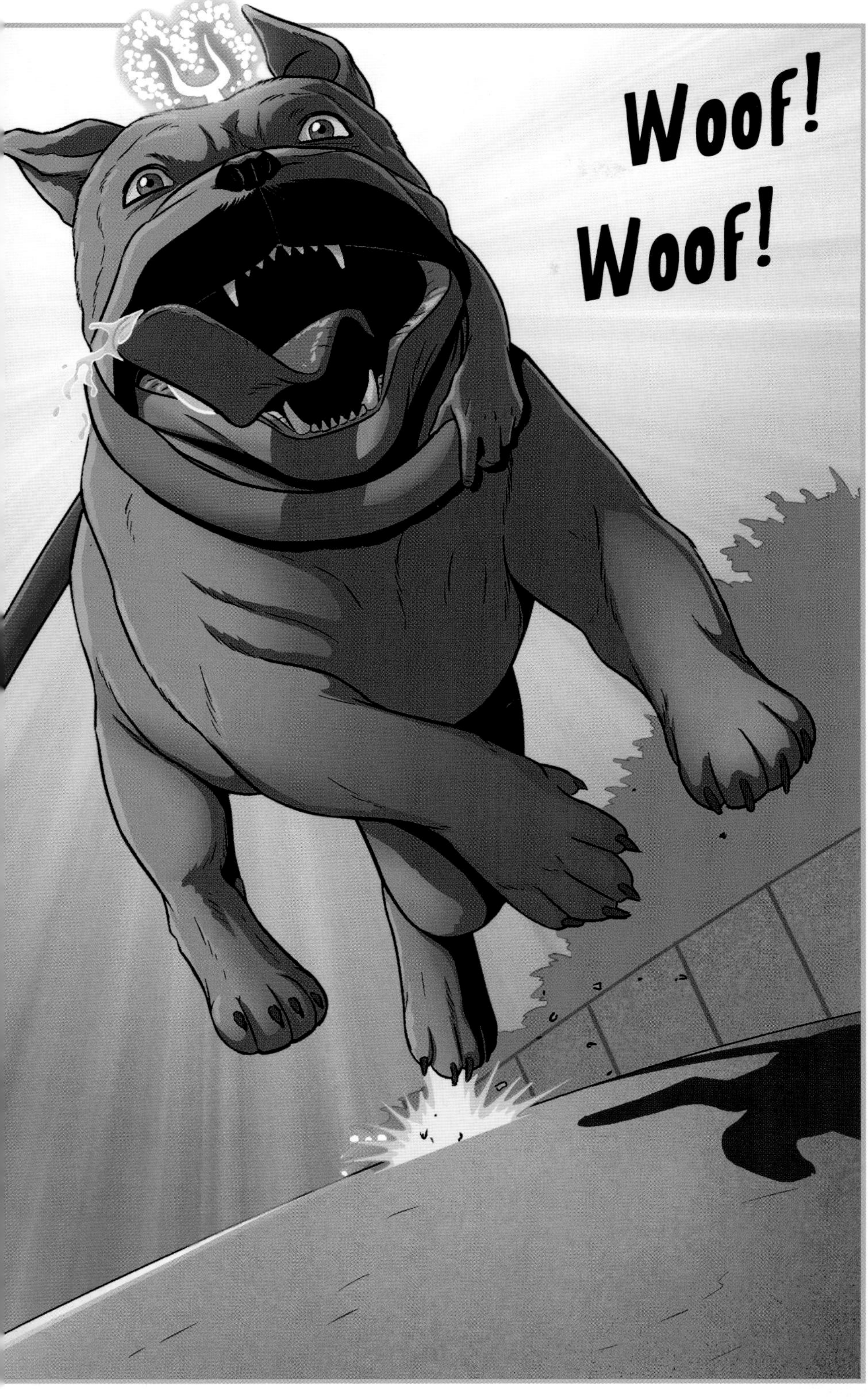
Woof!
Woof!

Kamala's family

Kamala lives with her mother, father, and brother in Jersey City. Kamala keeps her powers secret. Her family does not know she is a Super Hero.

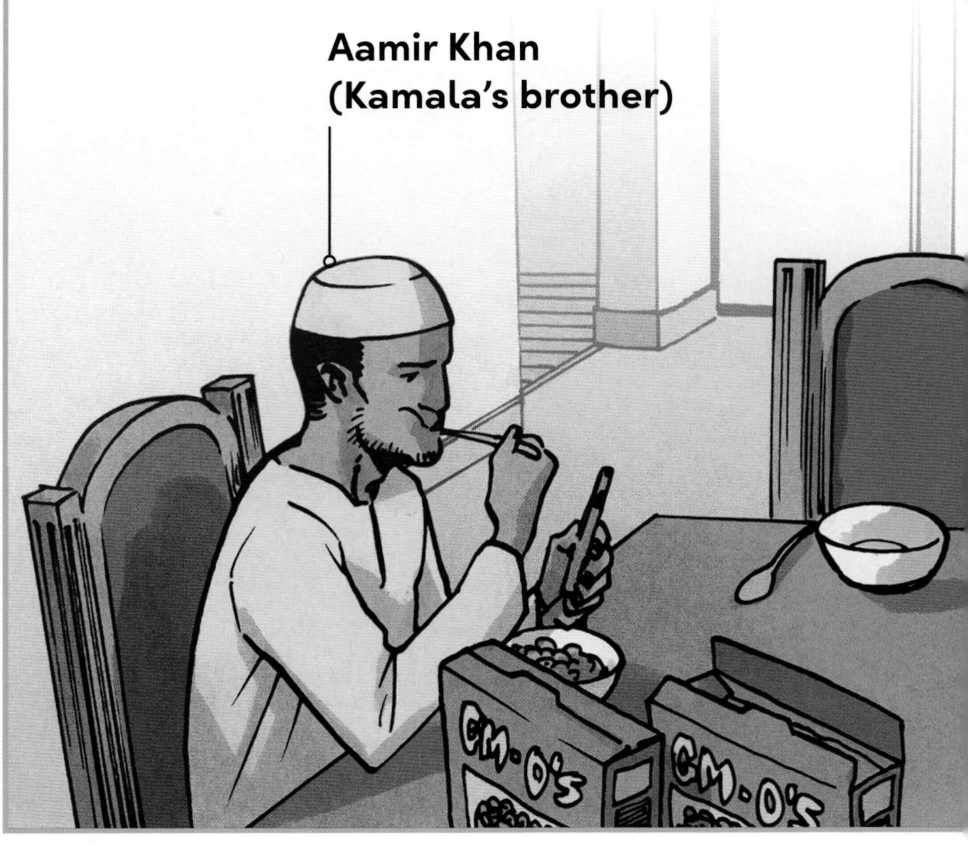
Aamir Khan
(Kamala's brother)
CM-O's
CM-O's

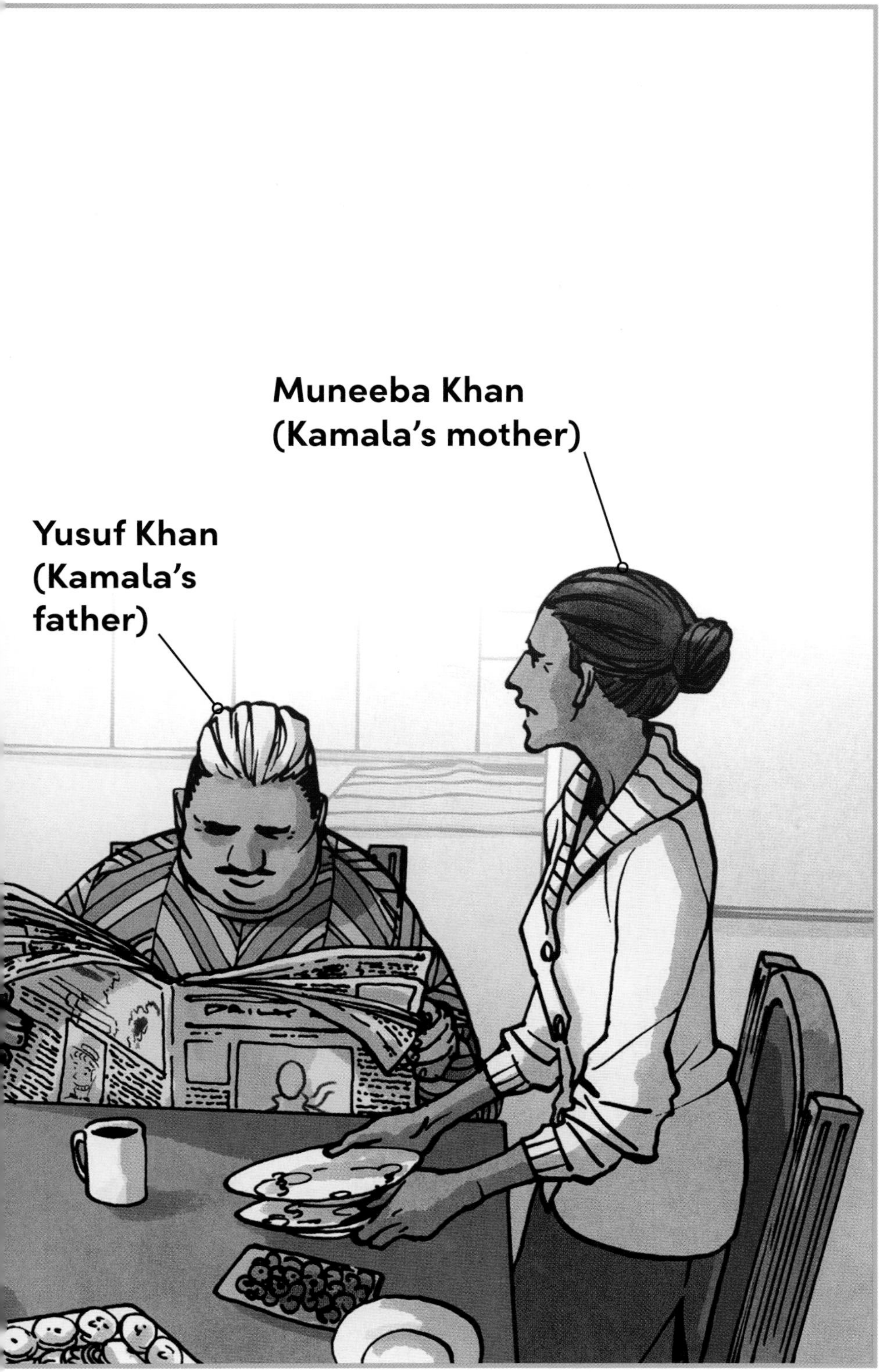
Muneeba Khan
(Kamala's mother)
Yusuf Khan
(Kamala's
father)

Jersey City

Kamala's parents moved to New Jersey before Kamala was born. Her mother, father, and brother were born in Karachi, Pakistan. Jersey City is Kamala's home. She will do anything to protect it.

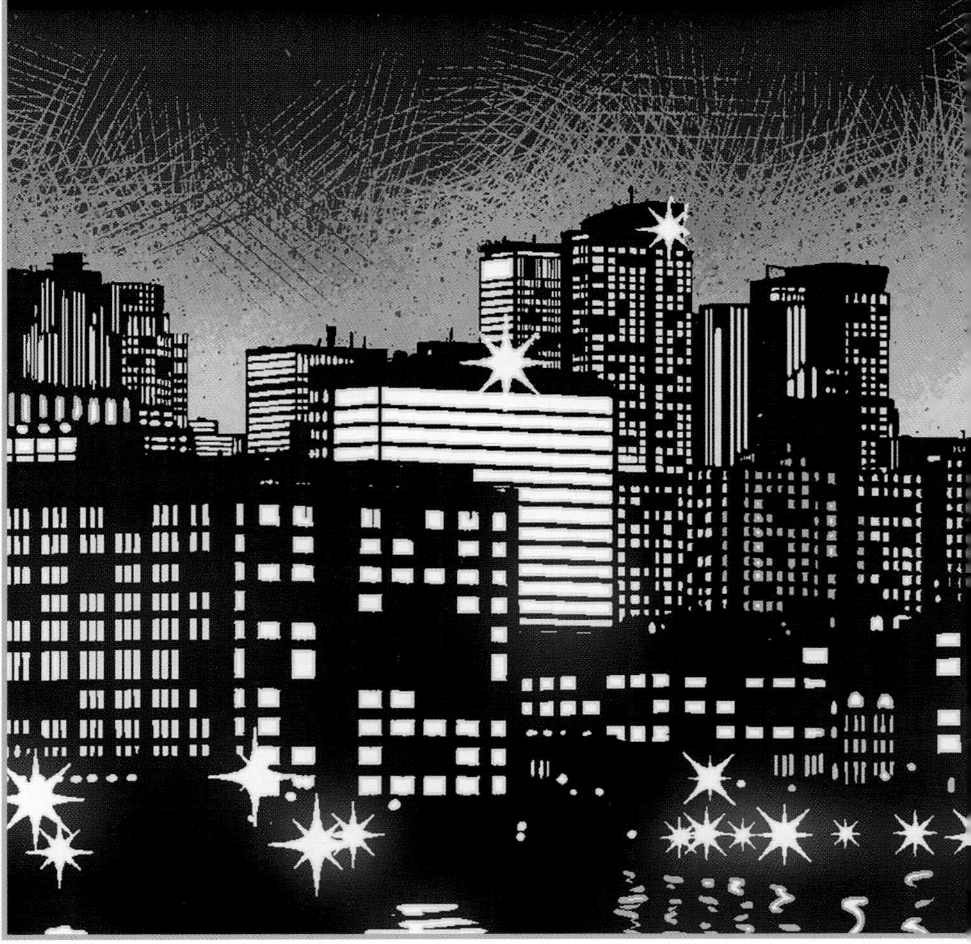

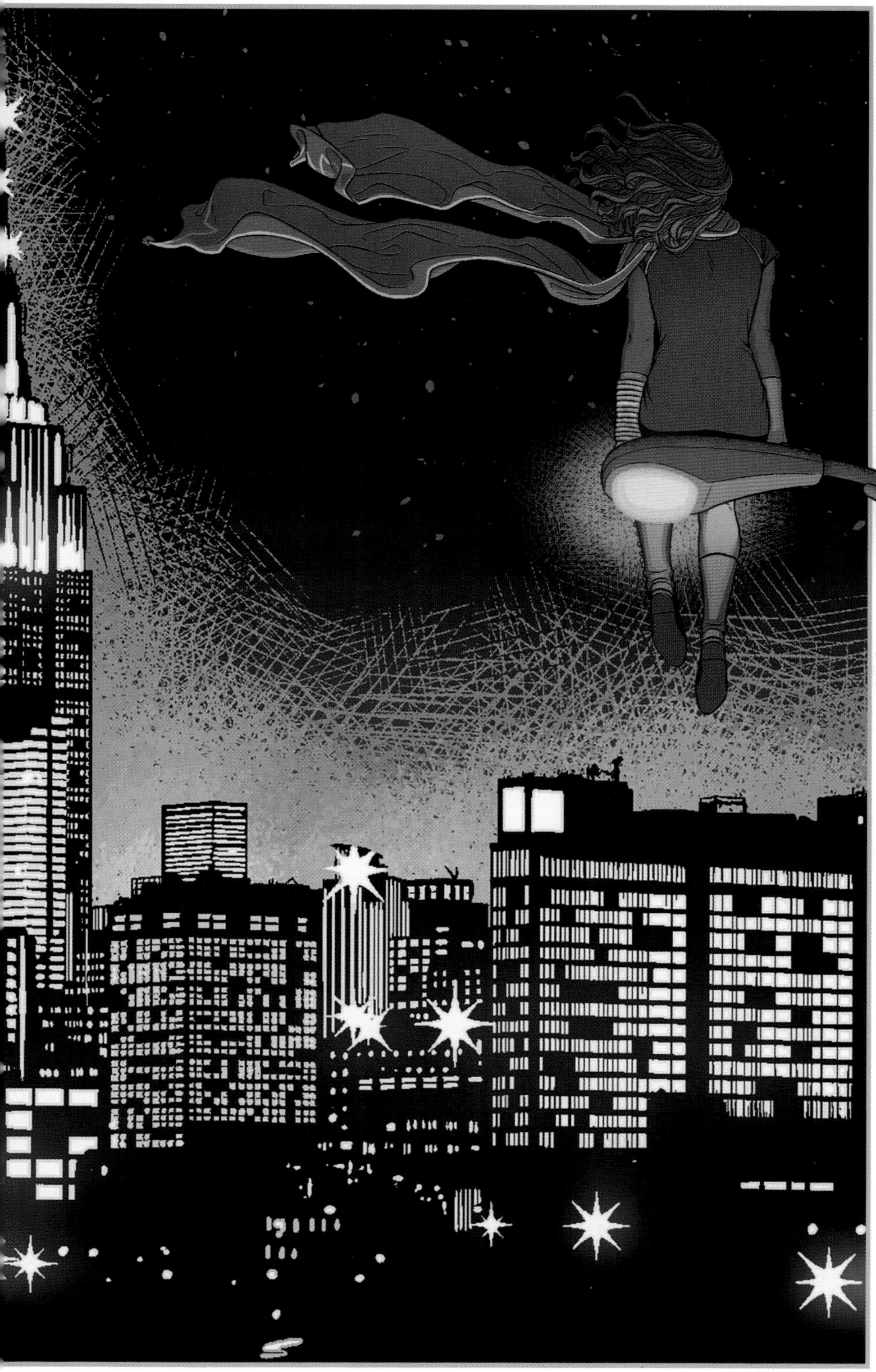

Fan fiction

Kamala writes fan fiction using the name Slothbaby. She writes about her favorite Super Heroes. Before she got her powers, Kamala also imagined what it might be like to be a hero!

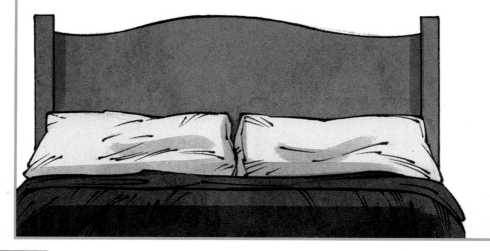

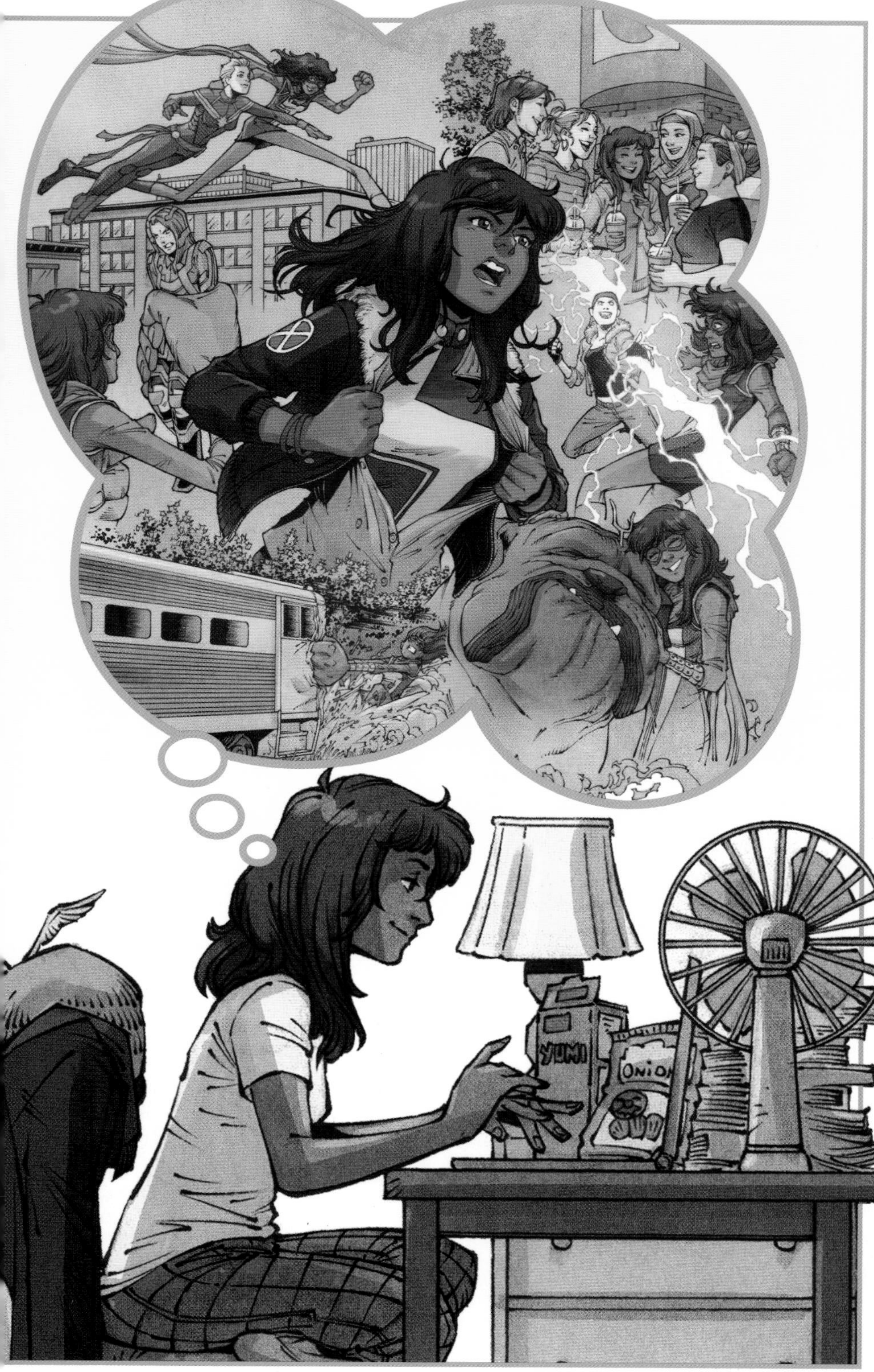
YUMI

Captain Marvel

Carol Danvers is the Super Hero Captain Marvel. Captain Marvel is really strong and she can also fly! She is Kamala's favorite Super Hero. Kamala chose her own Super Hero name because she is a big fan.

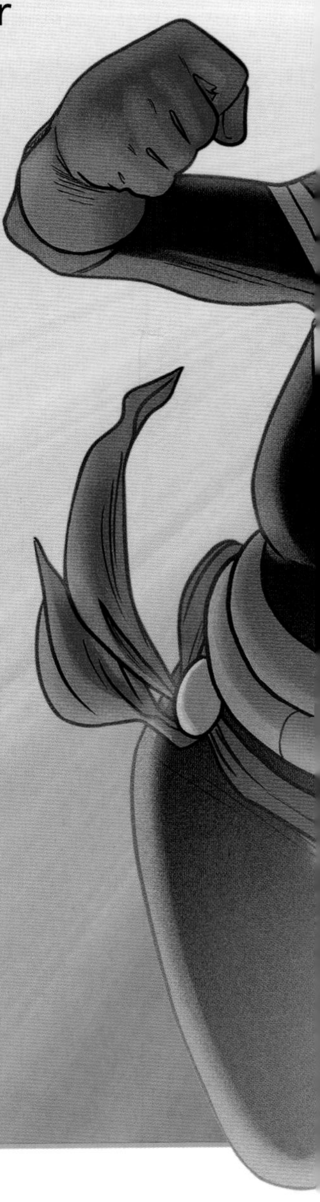

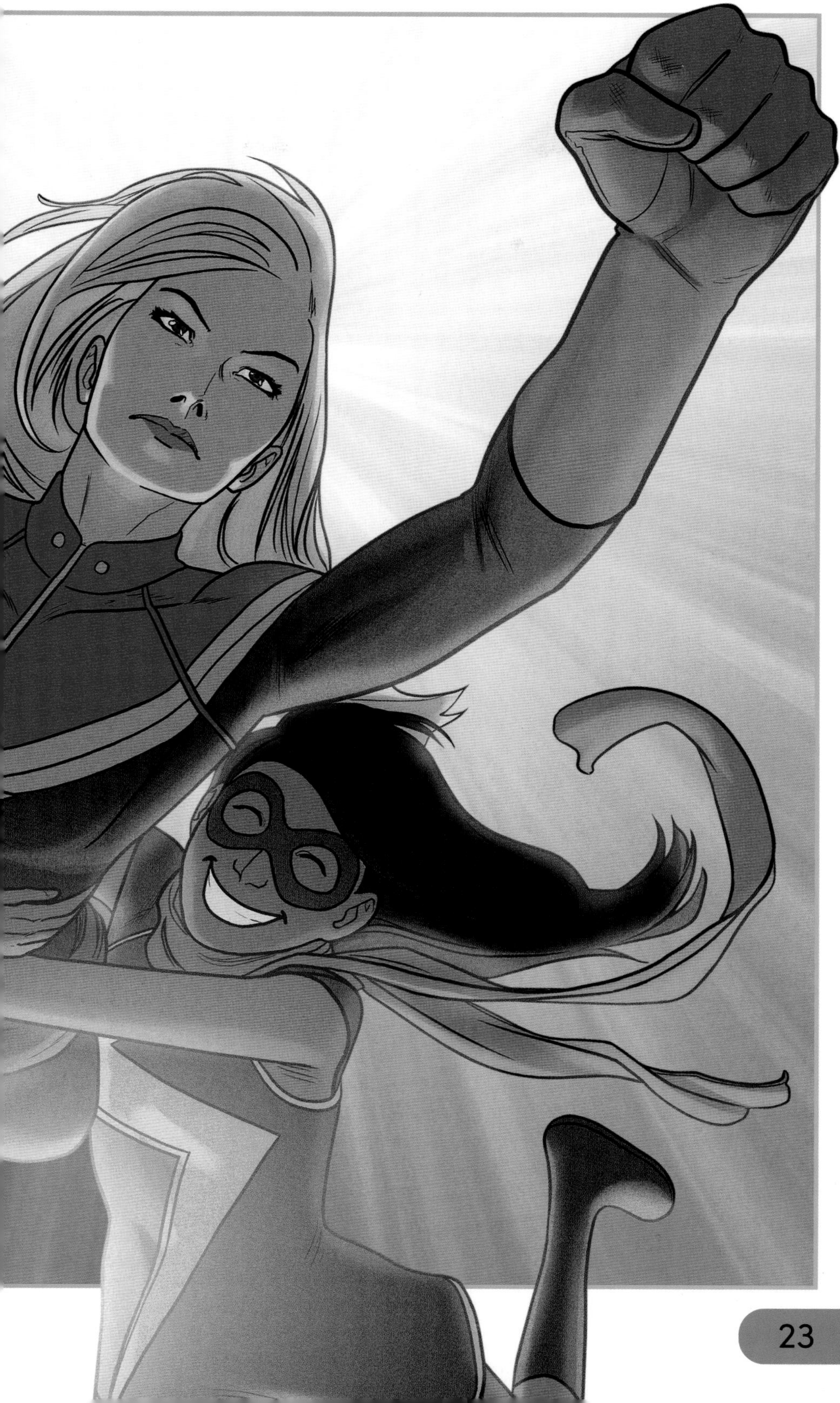

School life

Kamala is a student at Coles Academic High School. She is really clever, but being a Super Hero takes a lot of work. Sometimes Kamala is too tired to stay awake in class!

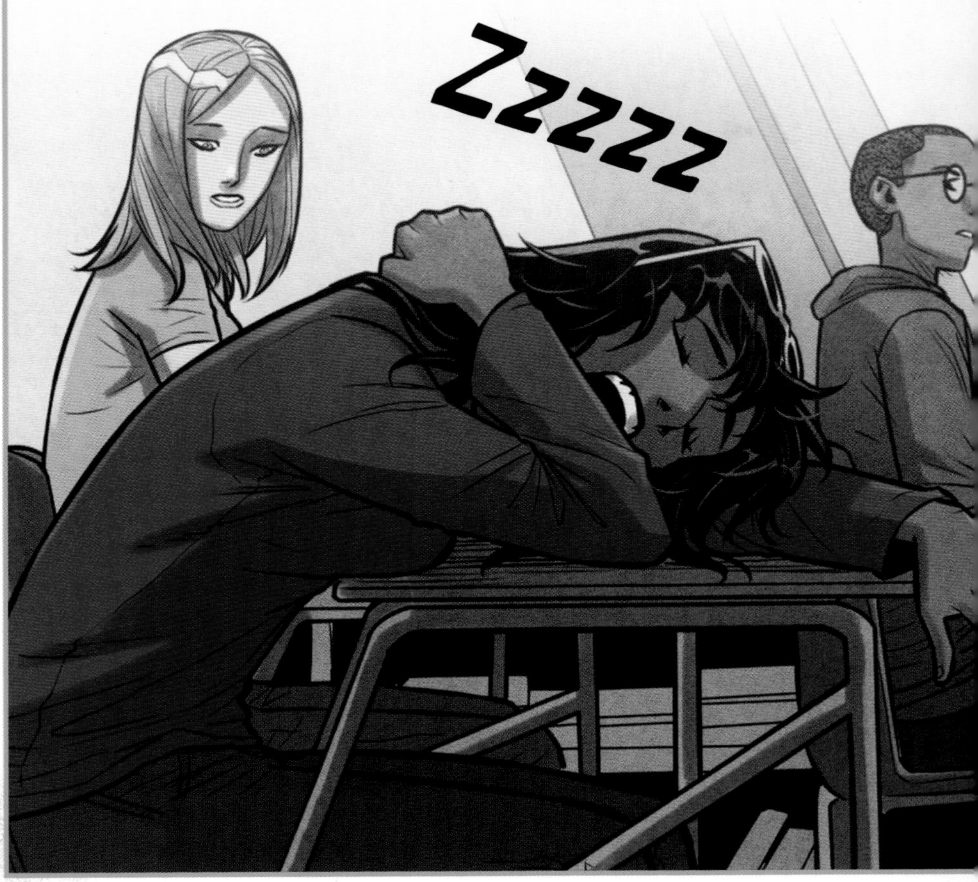
Zzzzzz

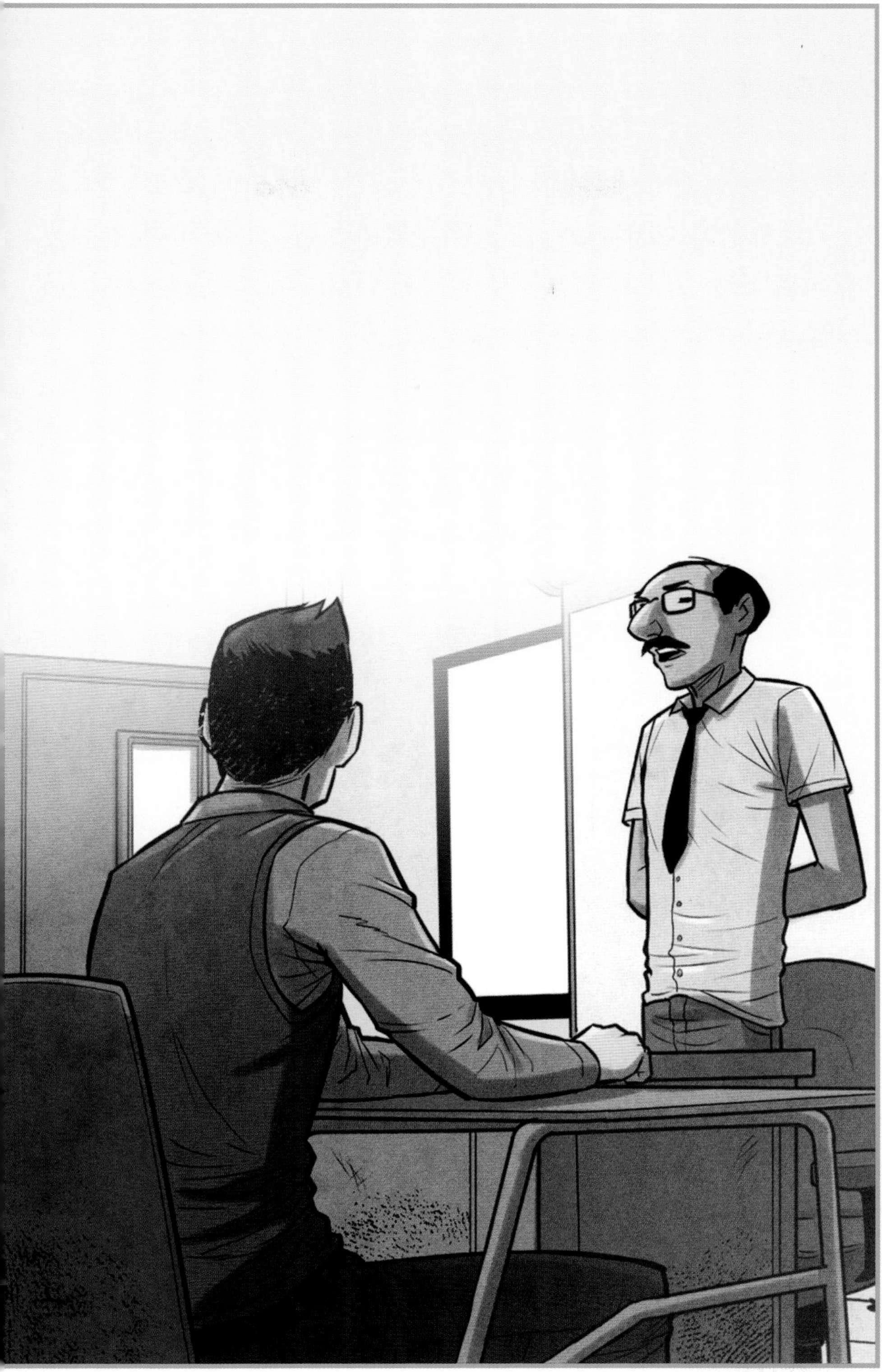

Nakia

Kamala met Nakia in kindergarten. Nakia is a practicing Muslim, just like Kamala. Kamala is grateful for her friends. She often feels she does not fit in at school. Nakia thought Ms. Marvel was trouble, until she found out she was her best friend!

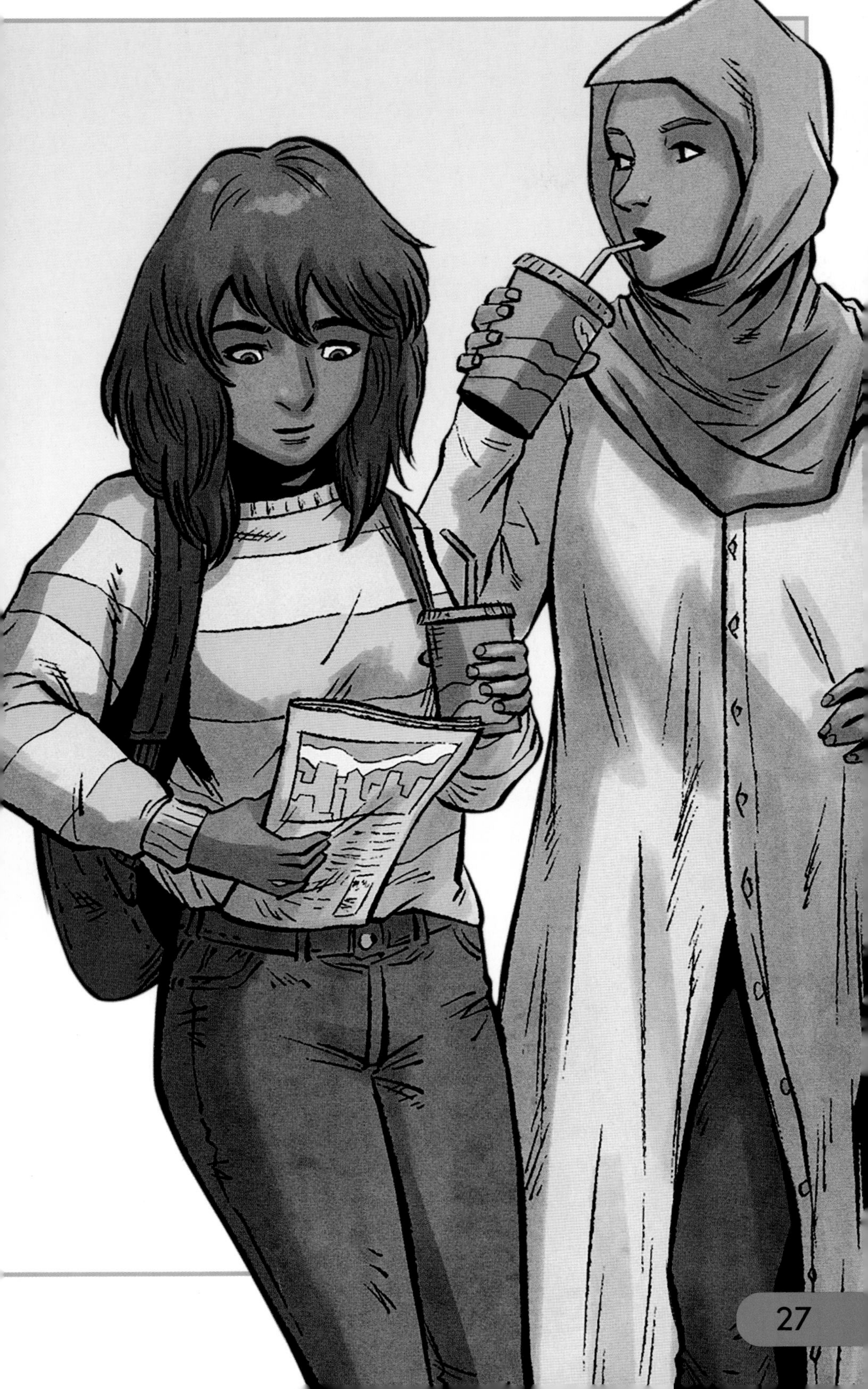

Bruno

Kamala met Bruno in elementary school, and they have been best friends ever since. They both enjoy writing fan fiction and playing computer games. Bruno helps Kamala keep her super-powers a secret and helps her create her stretchy costume and test her powers.

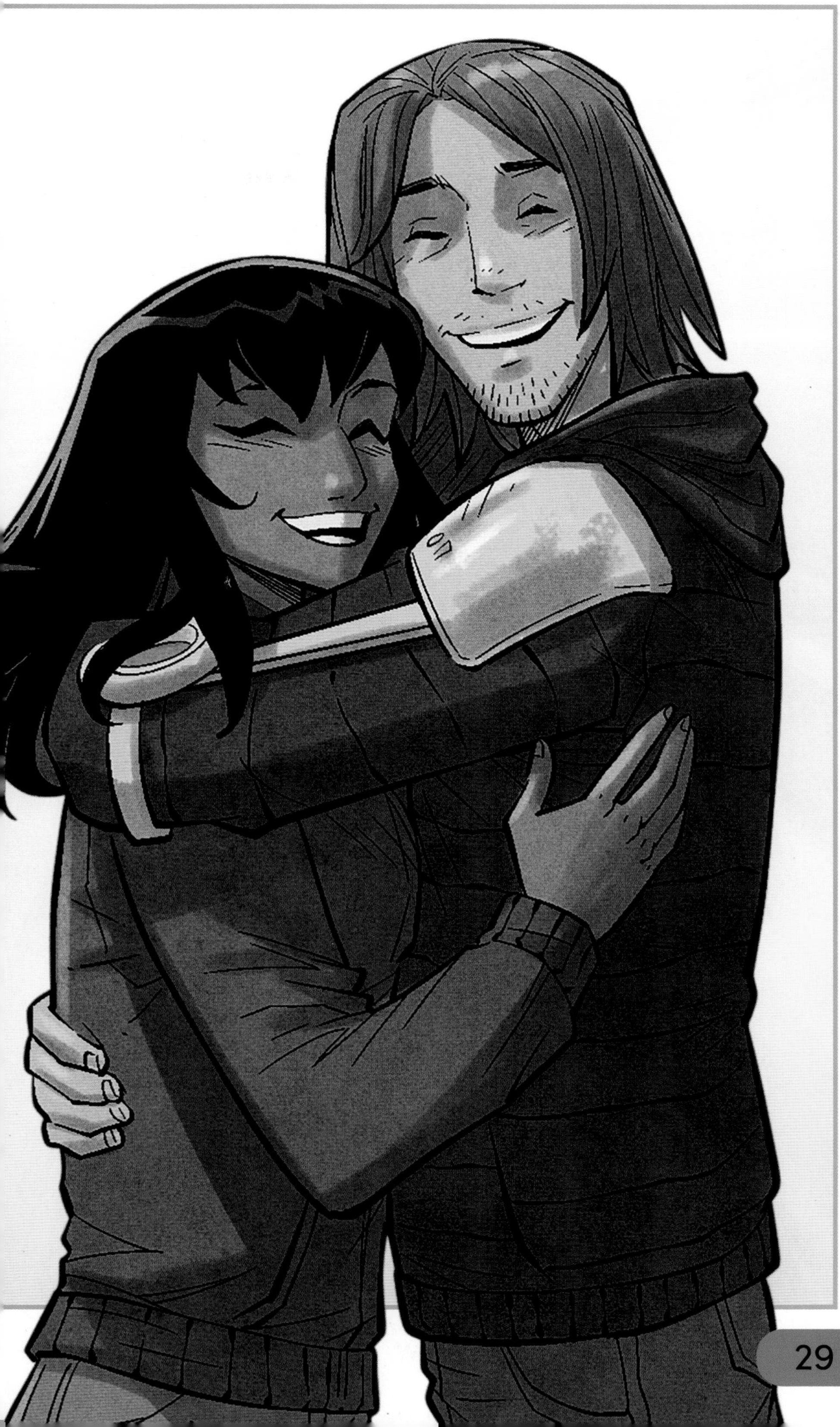

The Champions

Ms. Marvel leads a team of Super Heroes named the Champions. They work together to protect the world.

Viv Vision

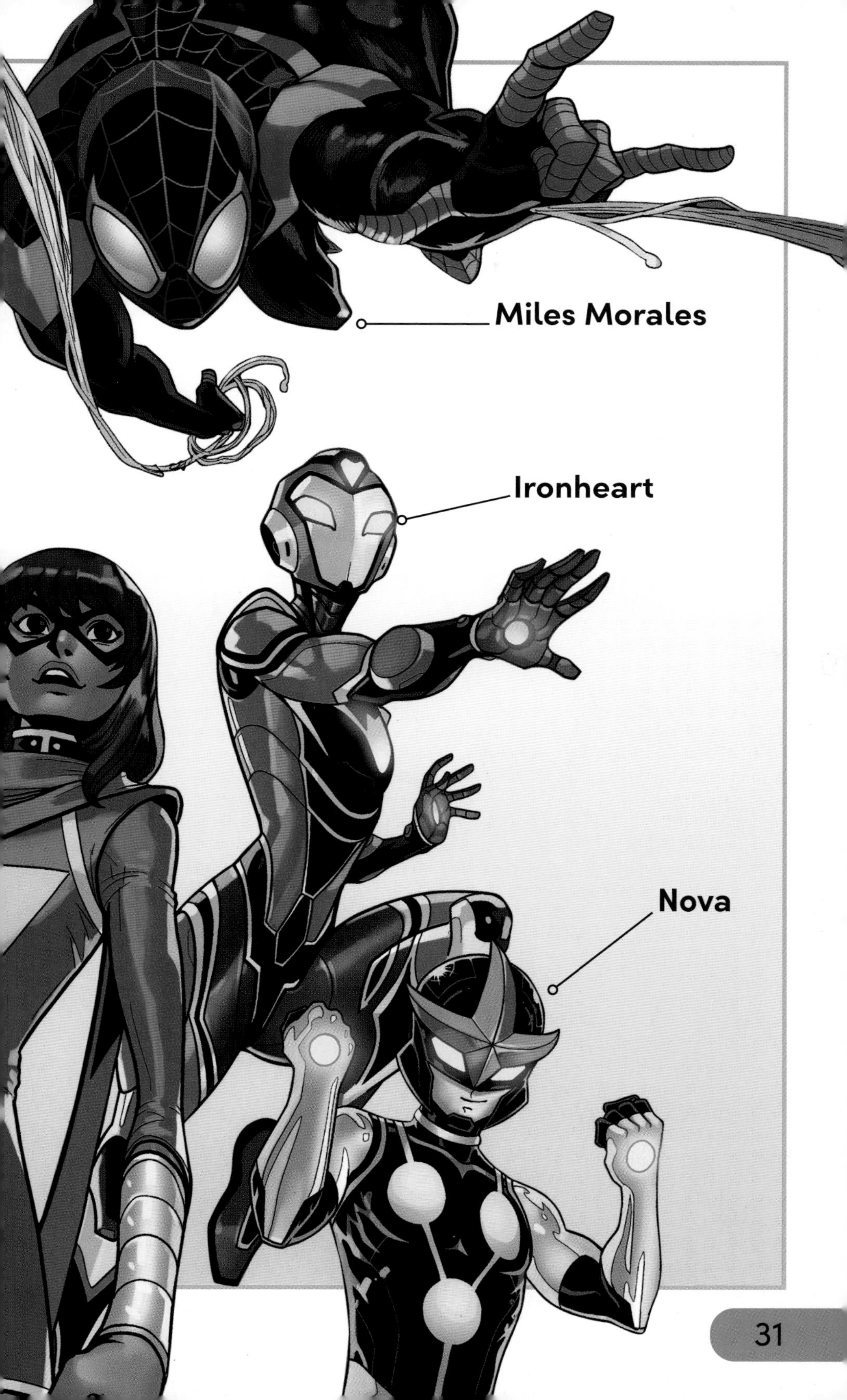
Miles Morales
Ironheart
Nova

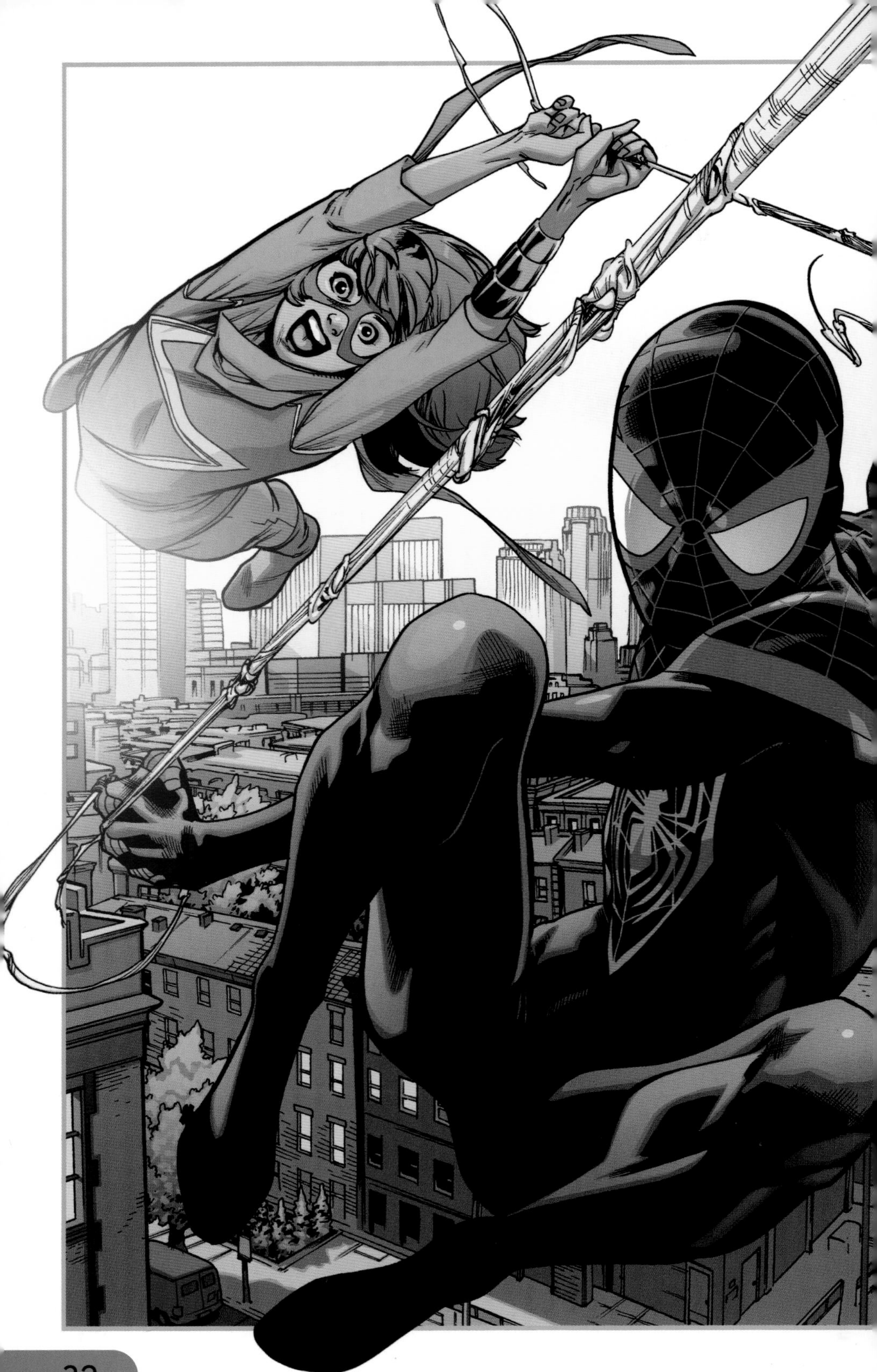

Miles Morales

Ms. Marvel is good friends with Miles Morales. Miles is a Super Hero named Spider-Man. Spider-Man can shoot webs from his wrists. He uses the webs to swing from buildings.

Kamran

Kamala's parents introduced her to Kamran. Kamran revealed he also had super-powers. He can change his skin to look like a crystal. Kamran can also use energy to create explosions.

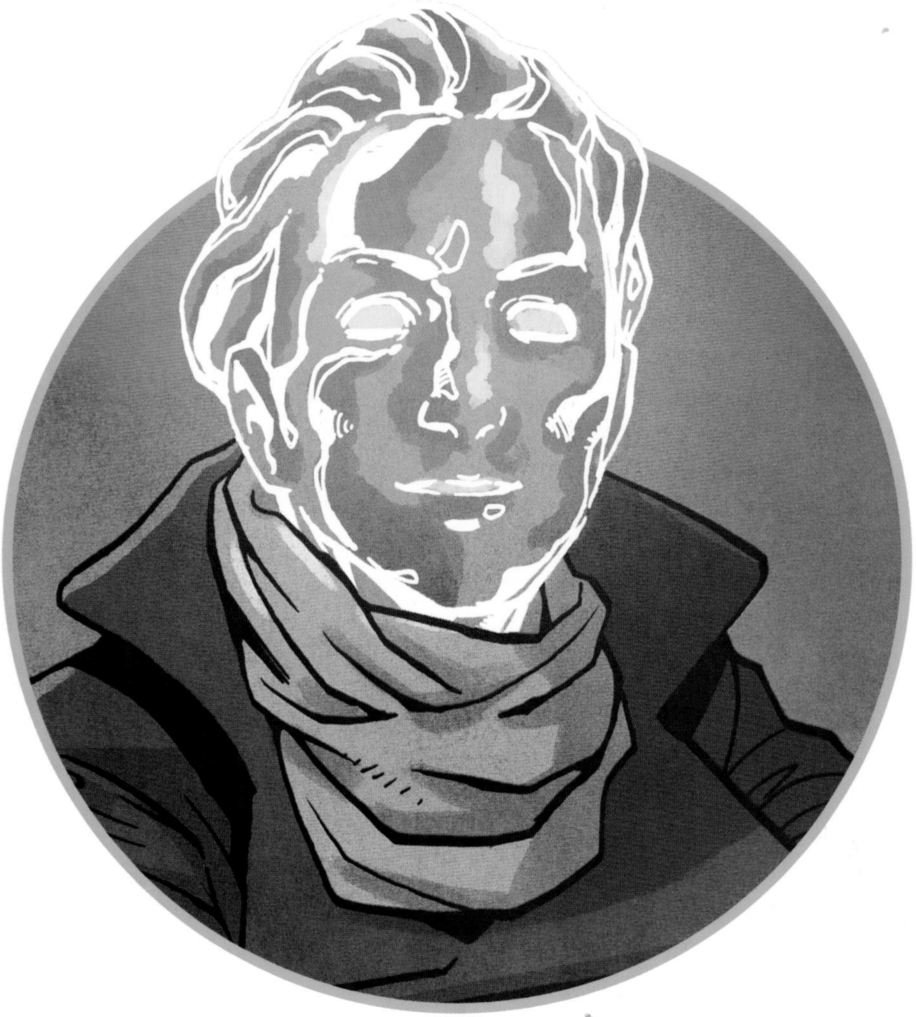

Kamala thought she had found a new friend. She soon discovered Kamran was working with a villain named Kaboom.

Lockdown

Becky St. Jude led a special team called the Carol Cadets. The team was supposed to protect Jersey City, but the power went to Becky's head. Kamala tried to stop Becky. Becky fought back and became a villain named Lockdown.

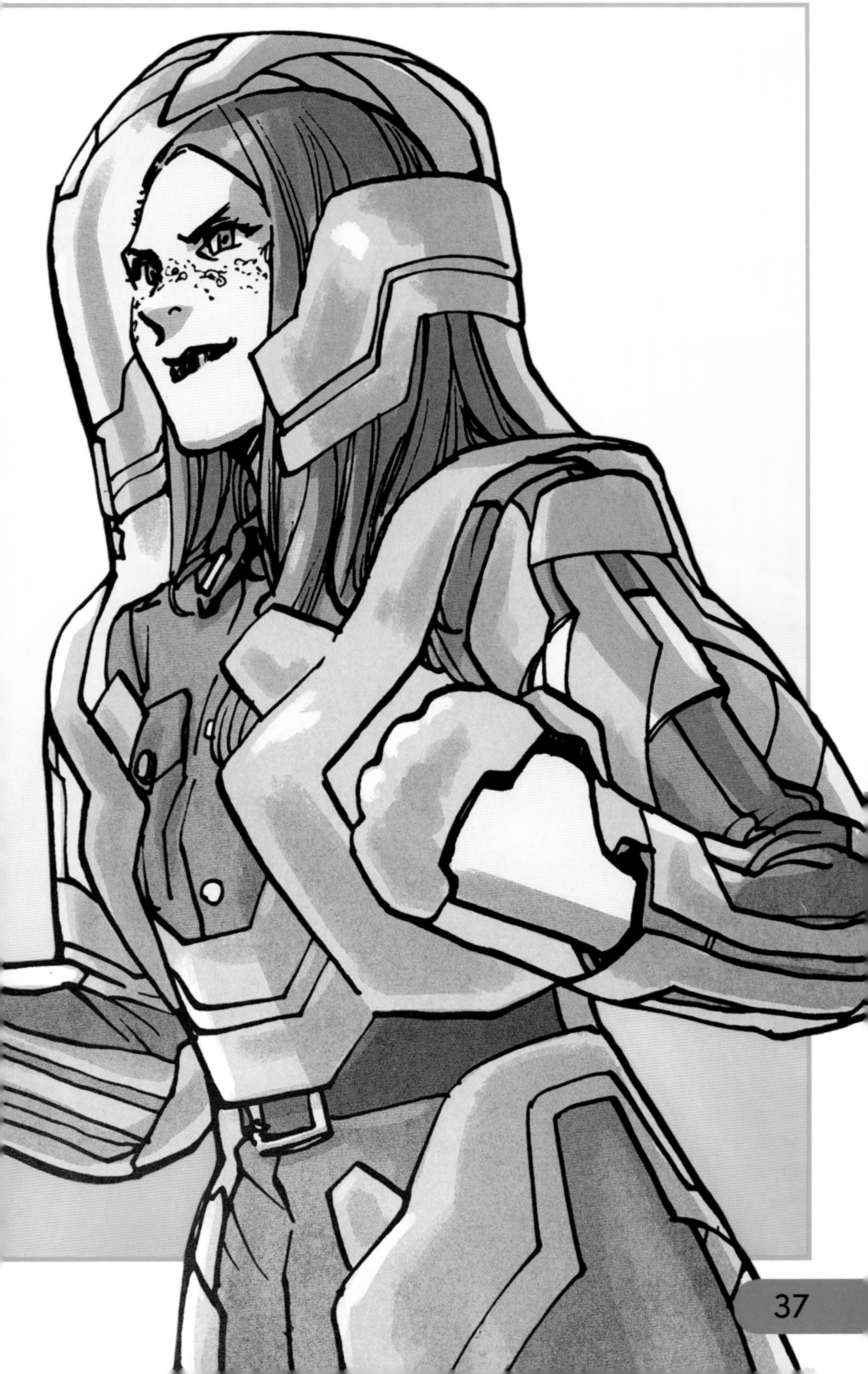

Warbringer

Warbringer is a dangerous space alien. He was in a deep sleep, but he woke up and made his way to Earth. He wants to spread violence in the world. Kamala teamed up with the Champions to defeat him.

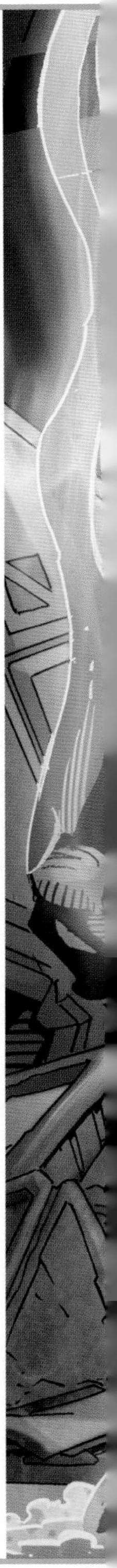

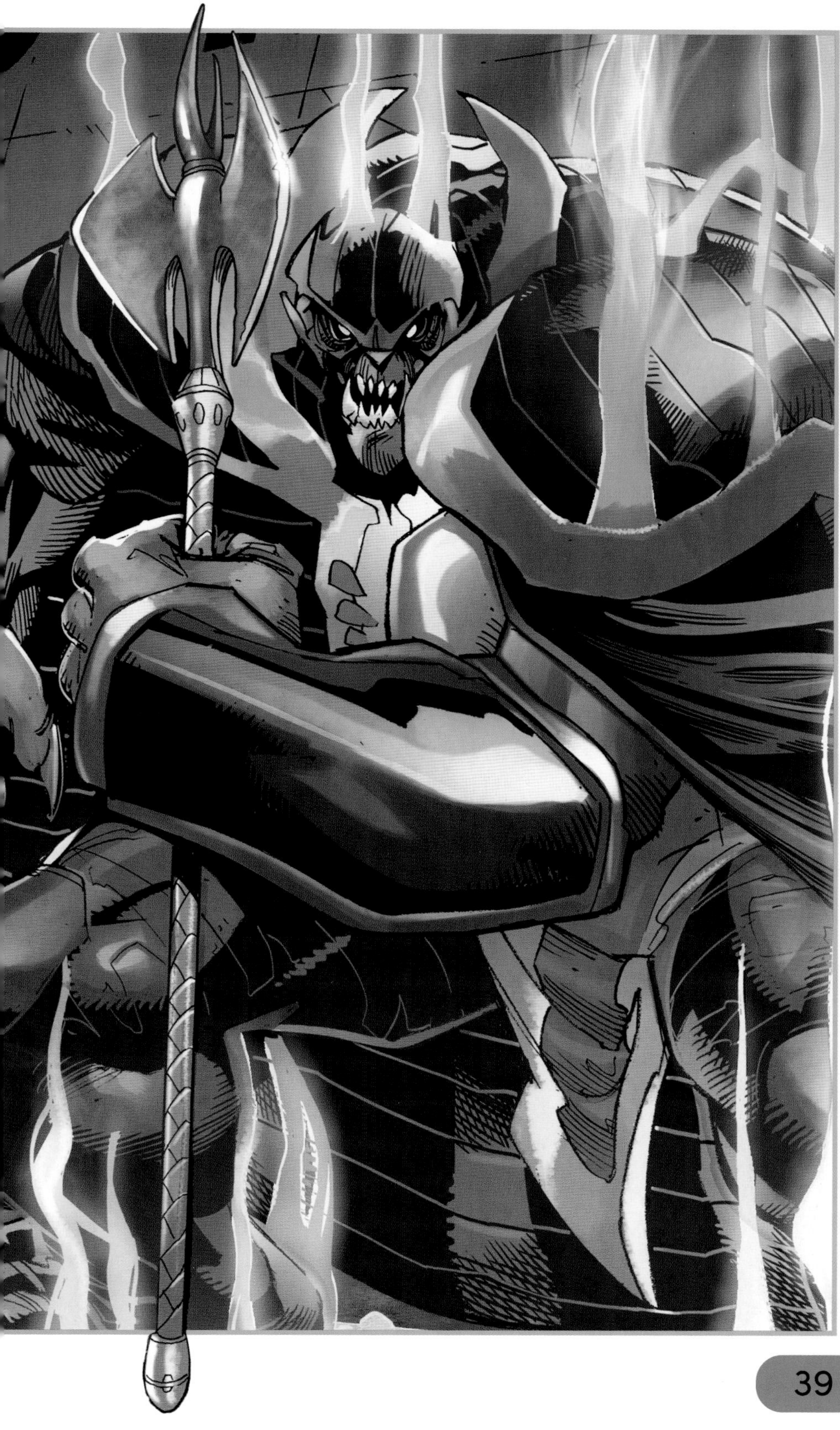

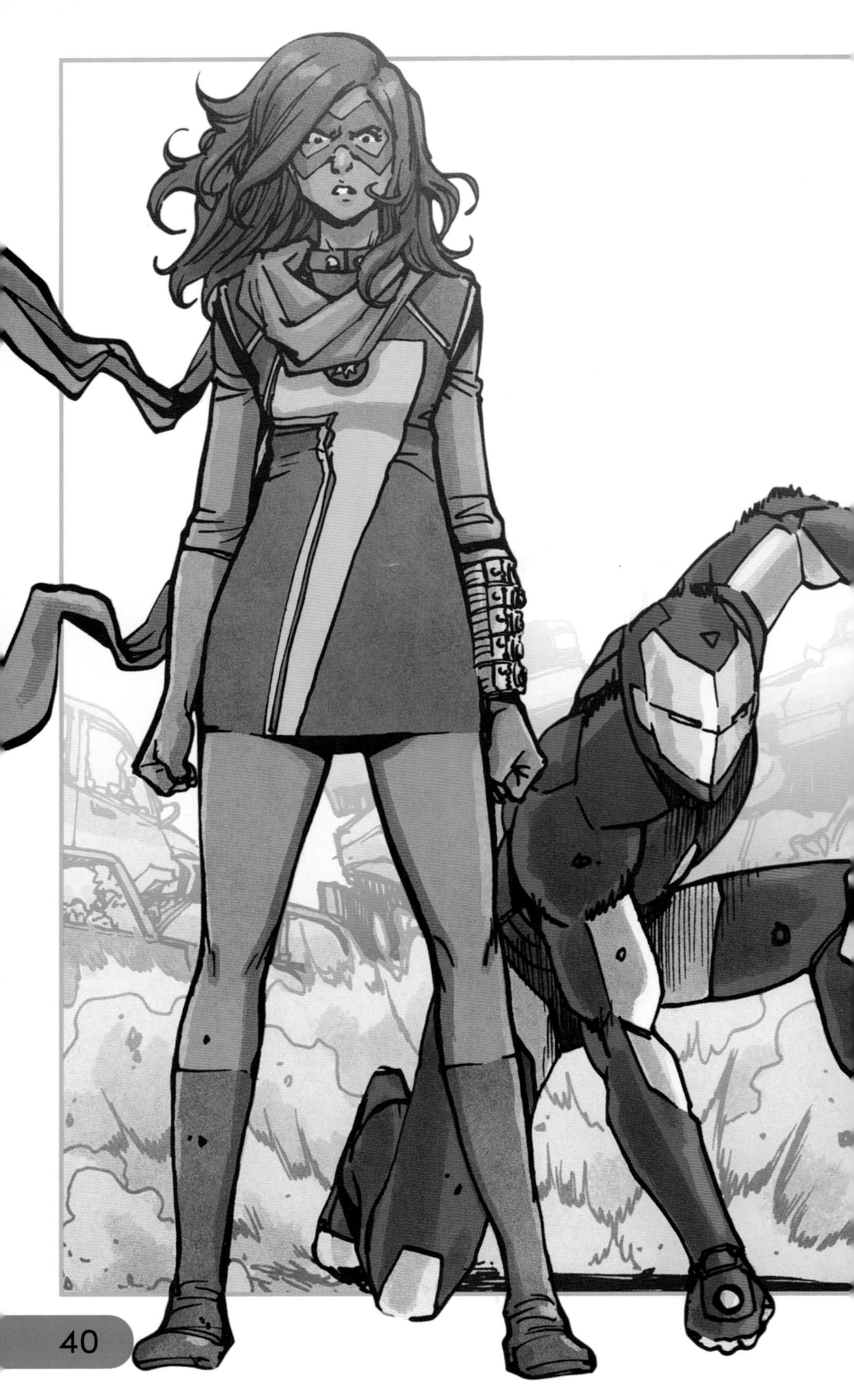

Iron Man

Iron Man is an amazing Super Hero. Iron Man helped Ms. Marvel protect Jersey City when it was attacked by a space alien named Warbringer.

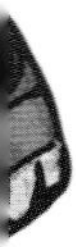

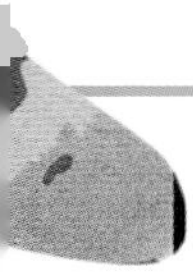

Doc.X

Doc.X was a computer virus that took on a physical form. It used the internet to discover Kamala's secrets. It threatened to reveal to the world that Kamala Khan is Ms. Marvel. Kamala's friends at school and in the game helped her defeat Doc.X.

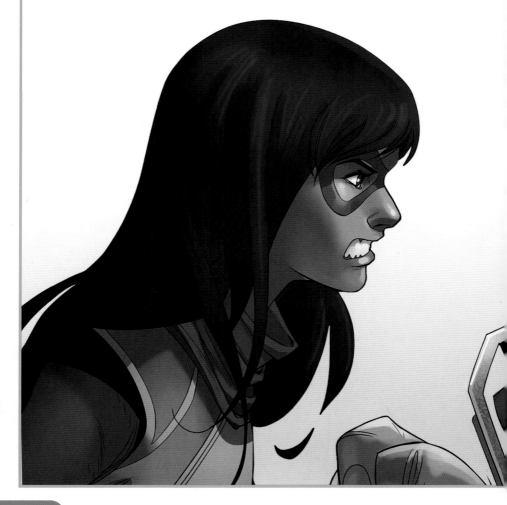

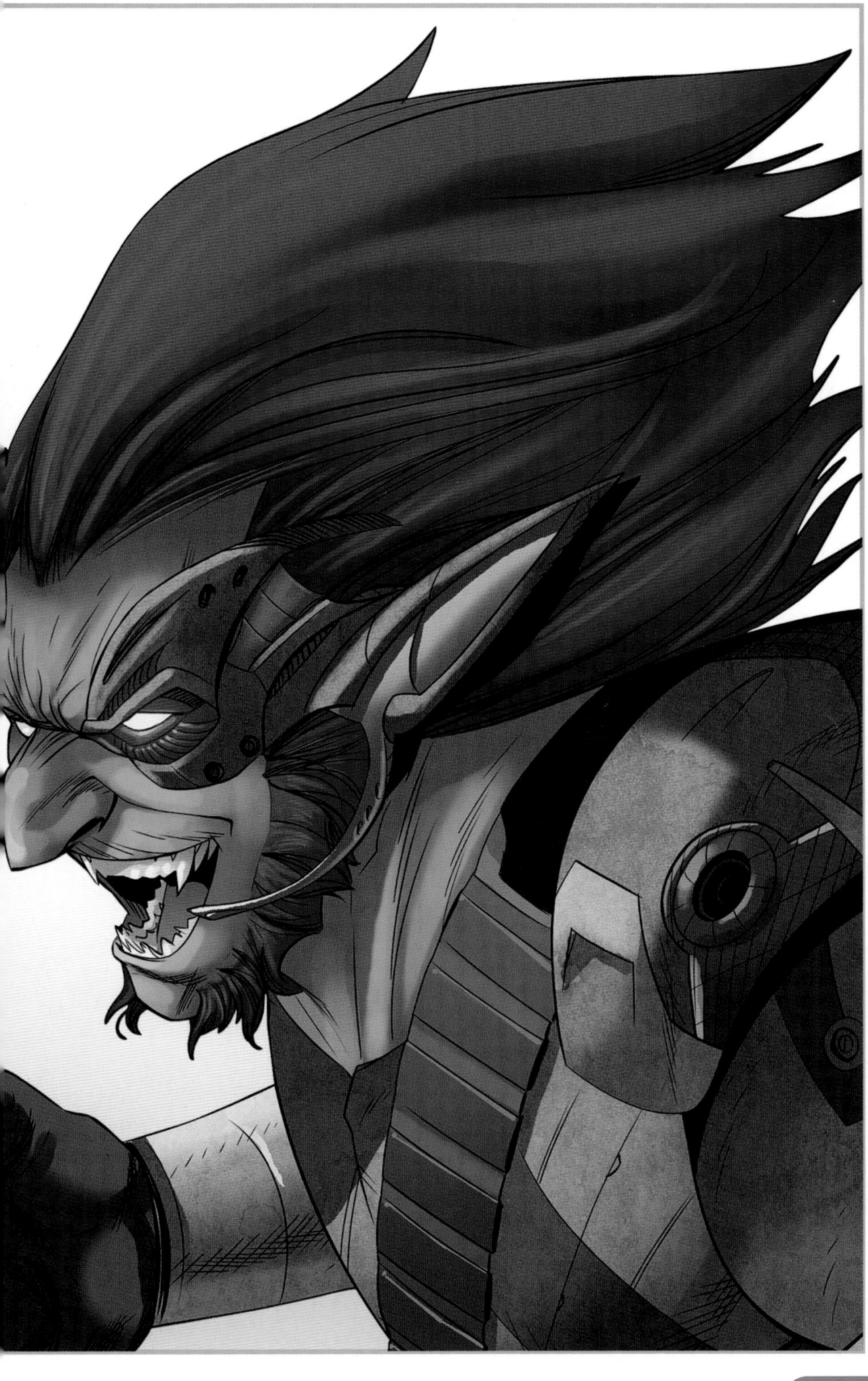

Saving the city

Kamala is not an ordinary teenager. Kamala is a hero! Whenever the people of Jersey City need help, they can count on Kamala Khan to save the day.

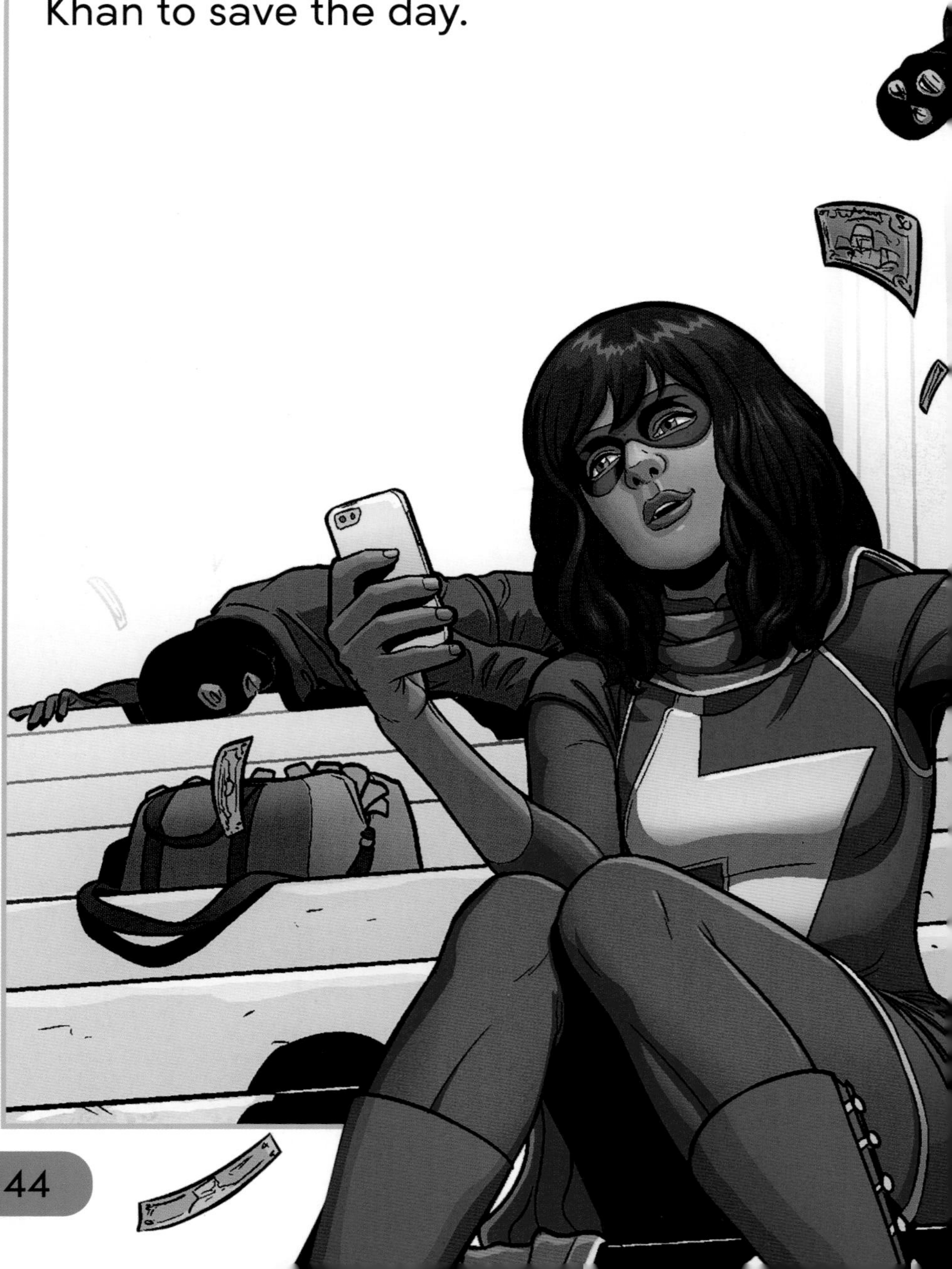

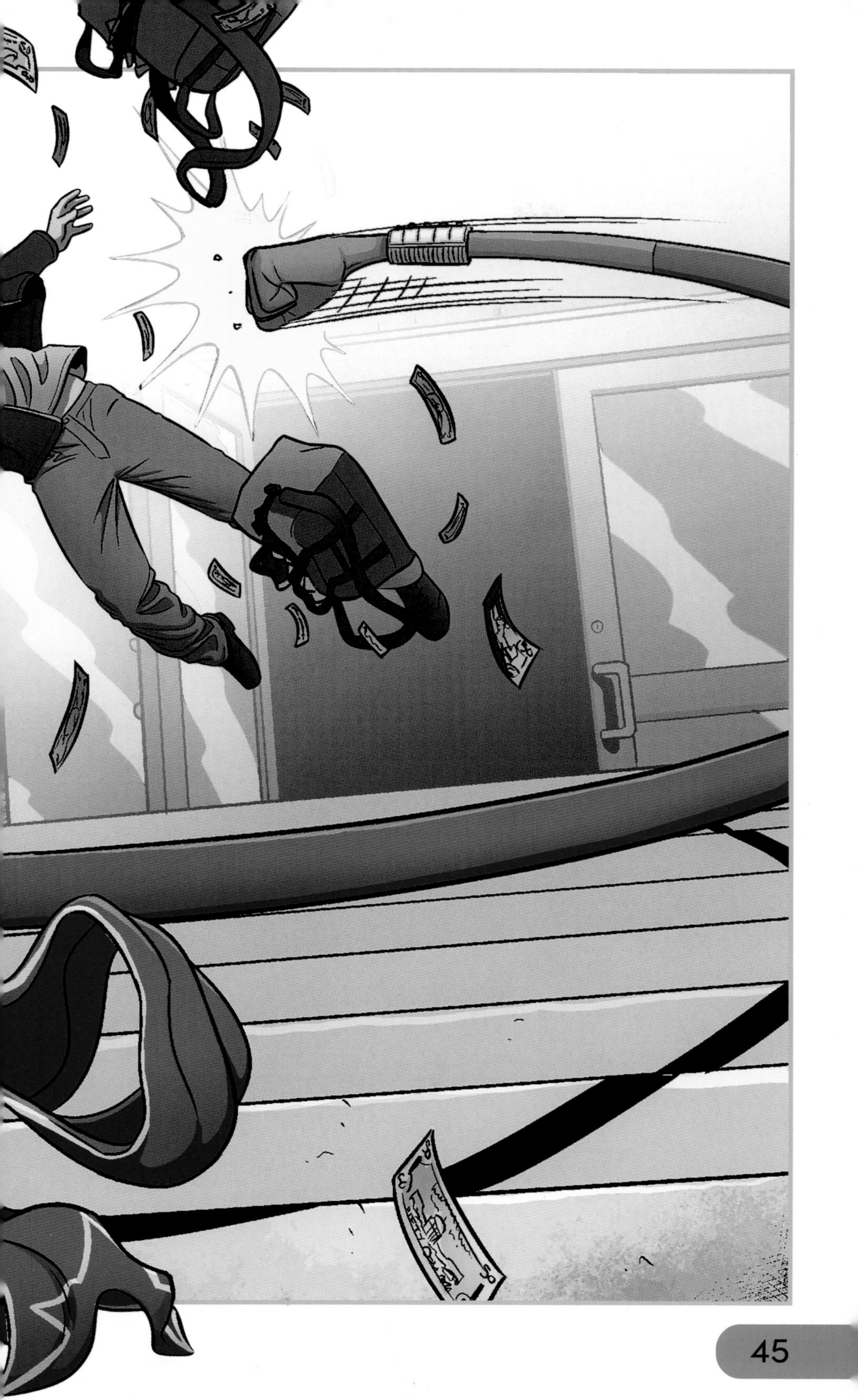

Glossary

engulfed
surrounded or covered completely

explosions
sudden bursts of energy that can
cause lots of damage

fan fiction
made-up stories written by fans

Inhuman
a human being who has been
changed by a special process and
has super-powers

Muslim
a person who follows the religion of
Islam

mysterious
something that is difficult to
understand

rebelled
resisted or went against someone
or something

teleport
to be transported through space or
distance

Index

Quiz

How well do you know Ms. Marvel?
Test your knowledge!

1. Where does Kamala live?

2. Where were Kamala's parents and brother born?

3. How did Kamala get her powers?

4. Kamala is a big fan of Captain Marvel. True or false?

5. Which one of Kamala's Super Hero friends can shoot webs from his wrists?

6. What is the name of the Super Hero team Kamala leads?

7. What is the name of Kamala's dog?

Answers: 1. New Jersey 2. Karachi, Pakistan 3. She was covered in a mysterious mist 4. True 5. Spider-Man 6. The Champions 7. Lockjaw